EJ
Urd

Urdahl, Catherine.

Emma's question.

$16.95

DATE			

Emma's Question

Catherine Urdahl • Illustrated by **Janine Dawson**

Charlesbridge

In memory of Mom, a true gift of God
    —C. U.

To my mum, who's a wonderful grandma for my daughter
    —J. D.

Text copyright © 2009 by Catherine Nelson-Urdahl
Illustrations copyright © 2009 by Janine Dawson
All rights reserved, including the right of reproduction
in whole or in part in any form. Charlesbridge and colophon
are registered trademarks of Charlesbridge Publishing, Inc.

Published by Charlesbridge
85 Main Street
Watertown, MA 02472
(617) 926-0329
www.charlesbridge.com

Library of Congress Cataloging-in-Publication Data
Urdahl, Catherine.
    Emma's question / Catherine Urdahl ; illustrated by Janine Dawson.
        p. cm.
    Summary: When Emma's grandmother, who takes care of her
after school and takes her out for bagels on Wednesdays, gets sick
and has to go to the hospital, Emma is afraid that she will die—
but she is also afraid to talk about her fear.
    ISBN 978-1-58089-145-5 (reinforced for library use)
    ISBN 978-1-58089-146-2 (softcover)
[1. Grandmothers—Fiction. 2. Sick—Fiction. 3. Worry—Fiction.]
I. Dawson, Janine, ill. II. Title.
PZ7.U638Em 2008
[E]—dc22   2007017185

Printed in Singapore
(hc) 10 9 8 7 6 5 4 3 2 1
(sc) 10 9 8 7 6 5 4 3 2 1

Illustrations done in pen and ink and watercolor on Montval
    watercolor paper
Display type and text type set in Elroy and Calligraph 810 BT
Color separations by Chroma Graphics, Singapore
Printed and bound by Imago
Production supervision by Brian G. Walker
Designed by Diane M. Earley

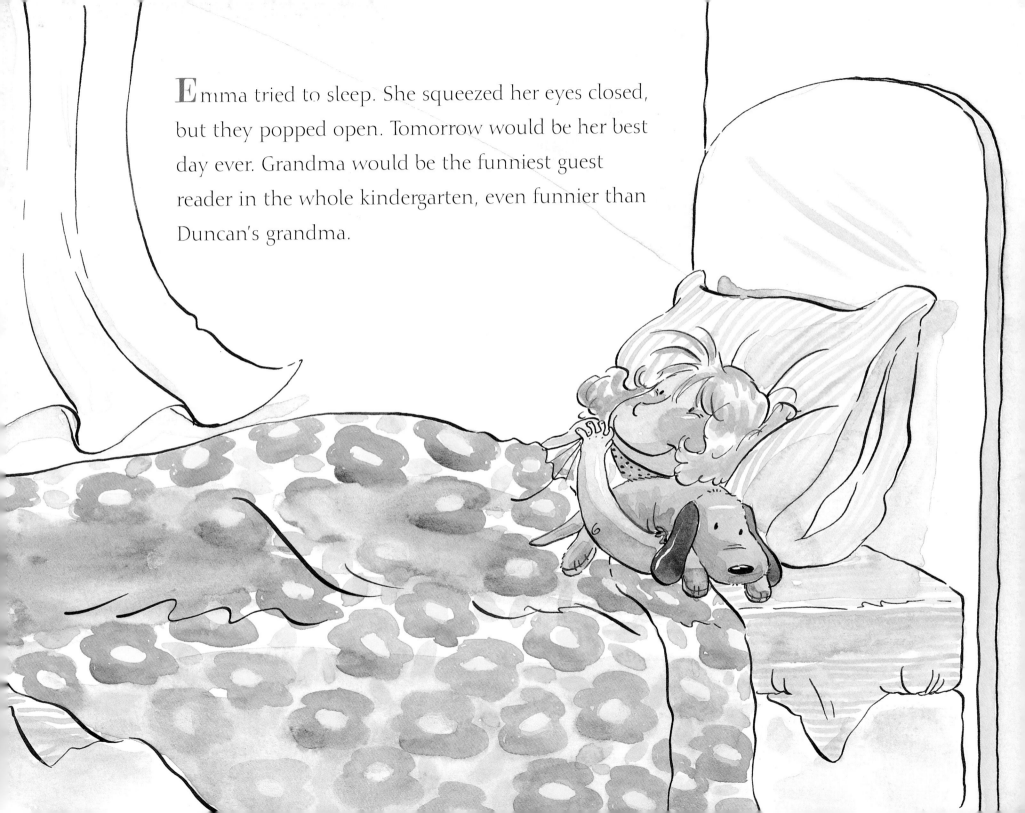

Emma tried to sleep. She squeezed her eyes closed, but they popped open. Tomorrow would be her best day ever. Grandma would be the funniest guest reader in the whole kindergarten, even funnier than Duncan's grandma.

Had Mama packed the book? Emma hopped
out of bed to check.

From the top of the stairs she spied
Mama on the phone. Mama's shoulders
shook. She was crying. This was not right.

"What are you doing up?" asked Daddy.

"Why is Mama crying?"

Daddy gave Emma a squeeze. "We just heard that Grandma is sick."

Emma had been sick lots of times. Last year she had the chicken pox, and no one cried. "She'll be better tomorrow. She's reading to my class. I'm turning the pages."

Daddy smiled a wobbly smile, but his eyes didn't crinkle a bit. "Sorry, Em. Grandma needs to stay in the hospital, where the doctors and nurses can take care of her."

Grandma must be really sick, thought Emma. A question scratched at her throat. She swallowed it down.

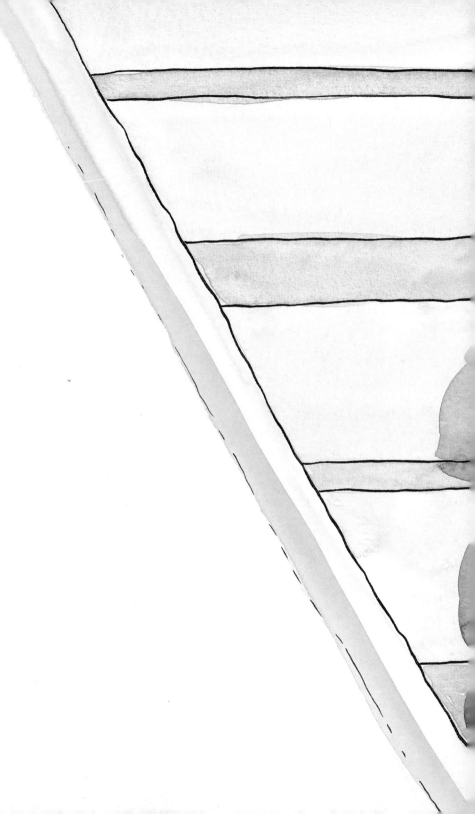

The next morning Emma counted the squares on her calendar. There were still ten days for Grandma to read before the end of kindergarten.

"How long will Grandma be in the hospital?" asked Emma.

Mama rubbed her eyes. "Maybe a week."

"But tomorrow is Wednesday!" cried Emma. "On Wednesdays Grandma takes me out for bagels."

Mama took Emma's hand. "I can take you."

Emma shook her head. "You don't let me pour the tea. You don't make up funny stories about the people at the next table. And sometimes you say, 'That's enough questions, Emma.'"

Mama smiled a skinny smile, but her eyes were puffy.

The question scritch-scratched in Emma's throat. But she was afraid to ask.

Emma's day was not good.

"Isn't your grandma reading today?" asked Duncan.

Emma shook her head. "She's sick. She had to go to the hospital."

Duncan's eyes popped wide open. "She must be *really* sick."

"Shut up," whispered Emma. Grandma did not like *shut up*.

At the art table Emma glued her dog's head upside down. At recess she couldn't jump rope past "Teddy bear, teddy bear, touch the ground." And at snack time she spilled her juice.

It was a terrible day.

When Emma got home, Mama was talking on the phone. "Could you take care of Emma after school tomorrow? I'd like to stay at the hospital a little longer."

"Grandma takes care of me—no one else!" cried
Emma. "I want to go with you."

Mama hugged Emma. "I'm sorry. Right now
Grandma can only have a few grown-up visitors. But
you can visit soon. The doctors just want her to rest."

Grandma only rested on Sundays. The question
clawed at Emma's throat. She clamped her lips together.

"Do you want to talk about Grandma?" asked Mama.

Emma took a deep breath. "Is Grandma . . . ?"
She peeked at Mama's sad face. "Never mind."

With Grandma sick everything was different. On Wednesday Emma ate toast for breakfast—it was crunchy and cold. On Thursday she tried to read her favorite book all by herself, but it was too hard. Worst of all, the question would not go away.

On Friday Mama was waiting by the door of the kindergarten, smiling. "We can visit Grandma this afternoon," she said.

As Emma walked through the hospital, she held
Mama's hand extra tight. In her other hand she
carried Chutes and Ladders—Grandma's favorite game.

"She might be too tired to play," said Mama.
Emma shook her head. "Grandma is never
too tired."

But Grandma was sleeping. Her face was gray-white, like kindergarten paste, and a web of tubes was taped to her arm.

Emma backed against the door.

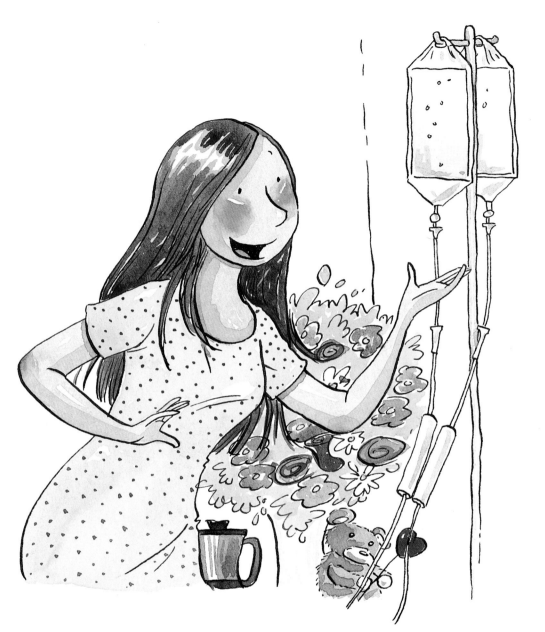

Mama pointed to a silver rack. "The tubes carry water and medicine from those bags into Grandma's body," she said.

Grandma opened her eyes just a little. "Em?"
Her voice was whispery. "I missed you."

Emma took a tiny step closer.

"It's okay," said Grandma. She nodded at the rack.

"Don't worry—that's just my dancing partner."

Emma tried to smile, but her lips were shaky.
She opened her mouth, then closed it again.
The room was quiet.

Grandma looked at Emma. "Do you
have something you want to ask?"

Emma shook her head. But the prickly question
scritch-scratched at her throat until it burned.
Before she could stop it, the question burst out.

"Are you going to die?"

"Emma!" cried Mama.

Emma tried to shrink into her dress. The room felt hot and shivery at the same time.

"That's a perfectly good question," said Grandma. She thought for a second. "Not today. I have a Chutes and Ladders game to play."

Emma smiled. "And not next Wednesday," she said. "You're taking me out for bagels."

"How about you bring the bagels to me? We'll make up funny stories about the nurses."

"And not next month," said Emma. "You're coming to my dance recital. And not next year—I might be getting married. But not to Duncan. He burps."

Grandma laughed a quiet laugh.
Then she reached for Emma's hand.
    Emma kicked her toe on the
floor. "Sometime?"
    "Sometime," said Grandma.
"But not now."

"Would you like to play your game?" asked Mama. Emma set up Chutes and Ladders. Grandma couldn't reach the spinner, so Emma spun for her.

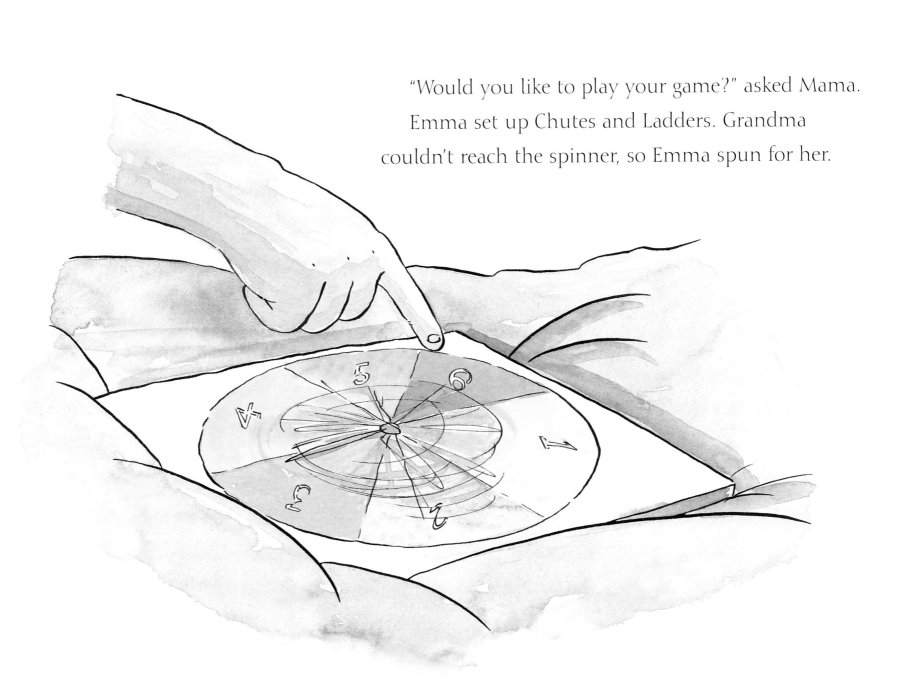

Grandma smiled a smile that made her eyes dance. And in that moment, Grandma was just the same.

Soon Grandma's eyes started to droop. "I need to take a break."

"Then I win!" said Emma.

"I guess you do," said Grandma.

Grandma never *let* her win. Emma scrunched her forehead. "We can finish tomorrow," she finally said.

"How very polite of you," said Grandma in her fancy-lady voice. "Before you go, please pour me a spot of tea."

Emma poured water into a plastic cup. "Here you are, Madam."